To Christina and Tiger

First published 2018 by Walker Books Ltd,
87 Vauxhall Walk, London SE11 5HJ

2 4 6 8 10 9 7 5 3 1

© 2018 Viviane Schwarz

The right of Viviane Schwarz to be identified as author
and illustrator of this work has been asserted by her in
accordance with the Copyright, Designs and Patents Act 1988

This book has been typeset in Trixie

Printed in China

British Library Cataloguing in Publication Data:
a catalogue record for this book is
available from the British Library

ISBN 978-1-4063-7103-1

www.walker.co.uk

ANIMALS

WITH

TINY

CAT

Viviane Schwarz

WALKER BOOKS
AND SUBSIDIARIES

LONDON • BOSTON • SYDNEY • AUCKLAND

CAT

MOUSE

ELEPHANT

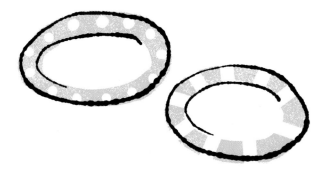

BIRD

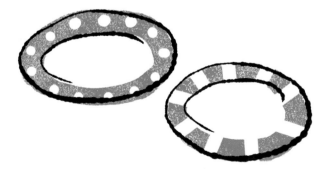

HORSE

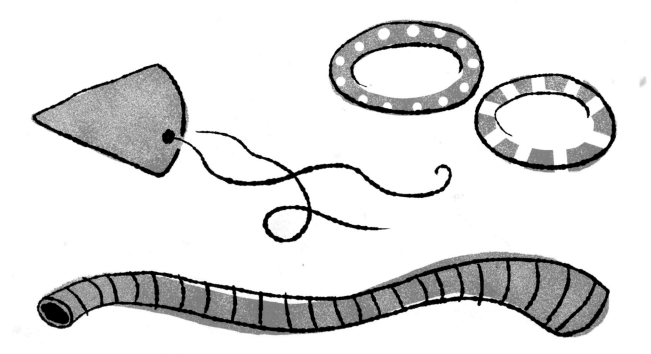

PORCUPINE

SNAKE

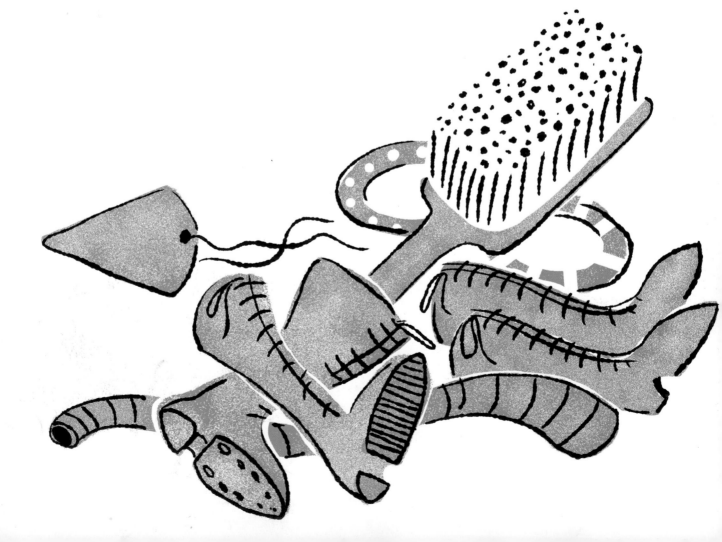

SPIDER

DRAGON

LION!